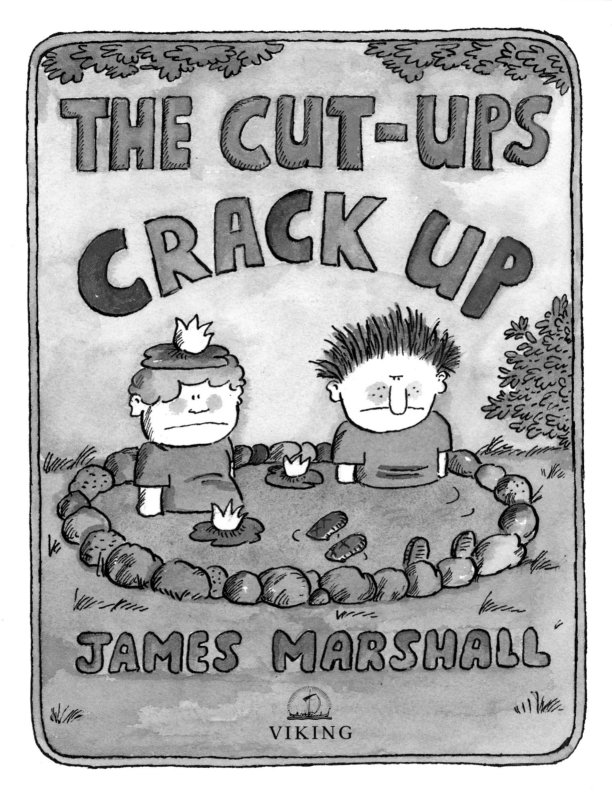

THE CUT-UPS CRACK UP

JAMES MARSHALL

VIKING

For Mervin Gorelnick

E
MAR

VIKING
Published by the Penguin Group
Viking Penguin, a division of Penguin Books USA Inc.,
375 Hudson Street, New York, New York 10014, U.S.A.
Penguin Books Ltd, 27 Wrights Lane, London W8 5TZ, England
Penguin Books Australia Ltd, Ringwood, Victoria, Australia
Penguin Books Canada Ltd, 10 Alcorn Avenue, Toronto, Ontario, Canada M4V 3B2
Penguin Books (N.Z.) Ltd, 182–190 Wairau Road, Auckland 10, New Zealand

Penguin Books Ltd, Registered Offices: Harmondsworth, Middlesex, England

First published in 1992 by Viking Penguin, a division of Penguin Books USA Inc.

1   3   5   7   9   10   8   6   4   2

Library of Congress Cataloging-in-Publication Data

Marshall, James, 1942–   The cut-ups crack up / by James Marshall.   p.   cm.
Summary: When Spud and Joe get behind the wheel of Principal
Lamar J. Spurgle's prized sports car, things soon get out of control. ISBN 0-670-84486-1
[1. Automobiles—Fiction.   2. Behavior—Fiction.   3. Humorous stories.]   I. Title.
PZ7.M35672Cuv   1992[E]—dc20   91-37964   CIP   AC

Printed in U.S.A.
Set in 16 pt Aster

Spud Jenkins and Joe Turner, a couple of rare cut-ups, were playing car crash.

"Look out for that truck!" cried Joe.

"The brakes don't work!" screamed Spud.

"Crash! Scrunch! Clank! Ker-pow! Clank! Smash!
Screech! Plunk! Crunch! Ker-pow!"
yelled the boys.
And they went flying right out of their seats.

Just then Mary Frances Hooley and the dreadful
Charles Andrew Frothingham happened by.
"Really, my dear," said Charles Andrew.
"Have you ever seen anything so immature?"

"Oh yeah?" cried Joe.

"It so happens our *real* car is in the shop!"

"Oh *please*," said Charles Andrew.

"You'll see, you'll see!" said Joe.

Mary Frances and Charles Andrew walked on.

"Why did you say we have a real car?" said Spud.

"I was exaggerating," said Joe.

"That guy really burns me up!

One of these days . . ."

Suddenly the boys got a tremendous scare.

A magnificent red sports car pulled up to the curb.

The boys' mouths dropped open.

"Look who's in it!" cried Spud.

"Oh my gosh!" cried Joe.

It was their old enemy, Principal Lamar J. Spurgle,
and his repugnant dog Bessie.

"Hello, lads," said Spurgle.

"Up to no good, I feel sure."

"What a car!" cried Joe.

"It's brand-new and all mine," said Spurgle.

"A present from the Board of Education
  for all my years of splendid work."

"Oh," said Spud and Joe.

"Don't even breathe on it," said Spurgle.

Spud and Joe watched as Lamar J. Spurgle
lovingly backed his new car into his driveway.

"I have an idea," said Joe.

"Don't even *think* it!" said Spud.

"We won't get in trouble," said Joe.

"Trust me."

Joe explained:

"If we could just get a picture of ourselves
   sitting in that car, Mary Frances
   and Charles Andrew would be completely fooled."

"Wow!" said Spud. "Where do you get your ideas?"

The boys went to Spud's house.
"Why do you want the video camera?"
said Spud's mom.
"It's for a school project," said Joe.

"Oh, sure," said Mom.

At Spurgle's house all was quiet.

"He must be taking his siesta," said Joe.

"Quick! Now's the time."

Spud tiptoed across Spurgle's lawn.

"The camera's rolling!" said Joe.

"Get in and wave."

Spud hopped into Spurgle's sports car.

But the moment he did . . .

A loud siren went off!

And a mechanical voice screamed,

"There is someone in this car! Help! Help!

Call 911! Foul play! Call the cops!"

"Turn it off!" cried Joe, hopping into the car.

"What's this button?"

Spurgle's car started up with a roar.
"Don't panic," said Joe.
But Spud's foot hit the accelerator,
and the car shot out of the driveway.

"I don't have a license!" cried Spud.
"Never mind that now!" cried Joe.

The sports car tore off down the street.
"Look out for that truck!" cried Joe.
"I can't find the brakes!" screamed Spud.

It was a narrow miss.
"You and your stupid ideas!"
said Spud.

At the corner of Maple and Elm they sailed by
an astonished Mary Frances and Charles Andrew.
"Just act casual," said Joe.

"What a neat car!" said Mary Frances.
"It's not so hot," said Charles Andrew
(who was really sick with envy).

Meanwhile, Spurgle's repugnant dog Bessie
tried to rouse her master from his siesta.
But Spurgle was sound asleep
and blissfully dreaming about his new car.
"Varoom!" he muttered, changing gears.

Va . . . *room!* roared the sports car
as the Cut-Ups raced down Main Street.
"The brakes must be here somewhere!" cried Spud.
At Main and Delancey they just avoided Joe's mom.
"That was close!" said Spud.

The Cut-Ups zipped all over town.

There were some pretty scary moments!

Finally, in the park, Spud located the brakes.

And they came to a complete stop.

Just then Charles Andrew and Mary Frances
strolled by.
Charles Andrew—who was very rich—
offered to treat the boys to ice cream.
"Huh?" said Spud.

"Miss Hooley and I will guard your sports car
while you're gone," said Charles Andrew.
"Gee," said Joe. "Sure!"
But while the boys were having their ice cream,
they heard a familiar sound.

Charles Andrew and Mary Frances had decided
to go for a little joyride.
"Wait! Wait!" cried Spud and Joe.
"That isn't *really* our car!
It belongs to Old Man Spurgle!"

"Huh?" said Charles Andrew.

"Stop this thing!" cried Mary Frances.

But Charles Andrew couldn't find the brakes either.

And off they flew.

Later in the day, Lamar J. Spurgle's doorbell rang.

It was the Board of Education and they were mad.
"You have behaved irresponsibly, Spurgle,"
said the head of the board. "Your sports car
has been seen breaking laws all over town.
We are taking it back—fork over those keys!"

Spurgle fell to his knees and pleaded for mercy.

"Don't take my car!" he cried pitifully.

"Lamar J. Spurgle is cracking up," whispered Spud.

"Sad," said Joe.

The boys were about to step forward and confess, when . . .

Charles Andrew and Mary Frances rolled up
to the curb and came to a complete stop.
"Out of gas," said Mary Frances.
"Arrest those little monsters!" cried Spurgle.
"They'll spend the rest of their lives
in summer school!"

Then Spurgle recognized his nephew Charles Andrew.

"I was just returning your car," said Charles Andrew.

"Some terrible cut-ups took it."

"What a fine lad," said Spurgle.

"All is forgiven," said the Board of Education.

"You may keep your car."

Spud and Joe decided to slip away unnoticed.

"How was your day?" said Spud's mom.

"Oh," said Spud, "it had its ups and downs."

And Spud's mom knew that could mean

all *sorts* of things.